BABA + RAY

10 Stories with Sathya Sai Baba teaching Ray, including Pictures for Coloring!

DOROTHEA CHAN

Clever Fox® PUBLISHING
Chennai • Bangalore

CLEVER FOX PUBLISHING
Chennai, India

Published by CLEVER FOX PUBLISHING 2025

ISBN: 978-93-6707-497-8

Luke + Wes with their little sister.

LORD GANESHA

DEDICATION

I dedicate this book to Baba and my sweet grandchild! .

CONTENTS

PREFACE

Ray is a special child too, just like her brothers Luke + Wes (separate book: Luke + Wes and their animal friends). She has the power of intention. As soon as she wishes for Baba with all her heart, He appears!

When she visits grandma she always says: "I love Baba." Grandma has this card deck with Baba pictures and quotes on it. She loves playing with those cards and loves watching Baba videos too!

In this book she summons Baba to share her joy she experiences in life. Then Baba usually gives her some important teachings to help her navigate through life!

May you all enjoy this book as much as I do!

PS: This is also a coloring book. The drawings were created by the author!

1
BEAUTIFUL CLOTHES

Today Ray is wearing her Indian clothes that Grandma brought back from her trip to Puttaparthi.

She misses Baba and calls out to Him: “Baba, please come and see what beautiful clothes I am wearing!”

Baba immediately appears and smiles at her. “Yes, Ray, you look beautiful in these clothes Grandma gave you!”

Baba goes on to teach her.

"All things are beautiful when seen through the eyes of love."

2
NATURE'S BEAUTY

Today, the family went on a nature hike. Ray loves nature and she wanted to share her happiness with Baba.

She called Him and He came.
Ray said to Him: "See Baba, how beautiful nature is!"

"Yes Ray" Baba replied. "I am pleased that it makes you happy to be in nature.

Ray, you can pray every day for all the beings in the world, asking God to see to it that they are happy too!" Ray thanked Baba for His teaching, and He spent some time with the family and then left.

Samastha Loka Sukhino Bhavanthu
Let all the worlds be happy
(and thereby all the beings in the worlds)

3
SWITZERLAND

In spring, the whole family travelled to Switzerland to visit relatives. Together they took the train and went up to the mountains.

Ray called Baba because she wanted Him to see the mountains. He appeared. Ray pointed to the mountains and said, "See Baba, the mountains have snow on top!"

Baba looked at the mountains and spoke:

"Ray, when you are a good girl and always speak the truth, your heart will get pure and white just like the snow!"

"It is the inner purity that matters, not the outer movement of lips."

4
INDIA

Ray travelled to India with her family. Indian people build so many temples to God. They went to visit a small one.

Ray liked the many depictions of God and called on Baba. Ray said to Him, "Look, Baba, this temple looks so nice with all these beautiful statues!" Baba replied: "Yes, Ray, I see! It is nice to build temples, but don't forget that God is inside you, Ray!"

"God is inside you.

God is in every word, in every deed and in every thought of yours.
Speak, do and think as it befits Him."

5
HIKE AROUND THE POND

The family went on an outing, walking around this beautiful pond. Her two brothers got into an argument and Ray didn't like it. She called Baba.

"Baba, Luke and Wes are fighting, I don't like it" she said. Baba replied, "Arguments happen sometimes. But be careful which words you use."

"Do not use poisonous words against anyone, for words wound more fatally than even arrows."

When Baba spoke the boys listened too, to what He said. They became peaceful and apologized to each other.

6
BACKPACK

The family went on a hike again and Ray's backpack was a bit big for her.

Ray immediately called Baba. As He arrived she said: "Baba, help me, this backpack is too big for me!"

Baba said, "Ray, it is good that you called me. Whenever your burdens are too great for you it is best to call on God."

"Give all your burdens to God. Be light and free. Have sacred faith. Without faith, there is no success in life."

Then Baba walked with them for a while and carried Ray's backpack!

LOVE IS MY FORM
SAI TOWERS FINE DINING EXPERIENCE

7
ANIMALS

Ray loves her white cat very much. Today they were outside in a beautiful scenery with colorful flowers. Ray called Baba: "Baba, I love my cat so much!" she said to Him.

Baba replied: **"Yes, Ray, I am very happy that you love animals, because they are all God's creatures!**

That is why it is important not to kill animals and eat them. It is cruel."

8
WATCH

Today Ray called Baba early in the morning: "Baba, the boys are wearing watches, I want a watch too!" she pleaded with Baba.

Baba answered: "Ray, the boys are quite a bit older than you. When the time comes you will get a watch. But know this: The word watch has this meaning:

WATCH	**WATCH YOUR WORDS**
ACTIONS	**WATCH YOUR ACTIONS**
THOUGHTS	**WATCH YOUR THOUGHTS**
CHARACTER	**WATCH YOUR CHARACTER**
HEART	**WATCH YOUR HEART**

So be careful which words you choose, when you talk. Make sure your actions are peaceful. You should have good thoughts. It is important to have a good character, like honesty, respect, etc.

Have love in your heart and compassion.

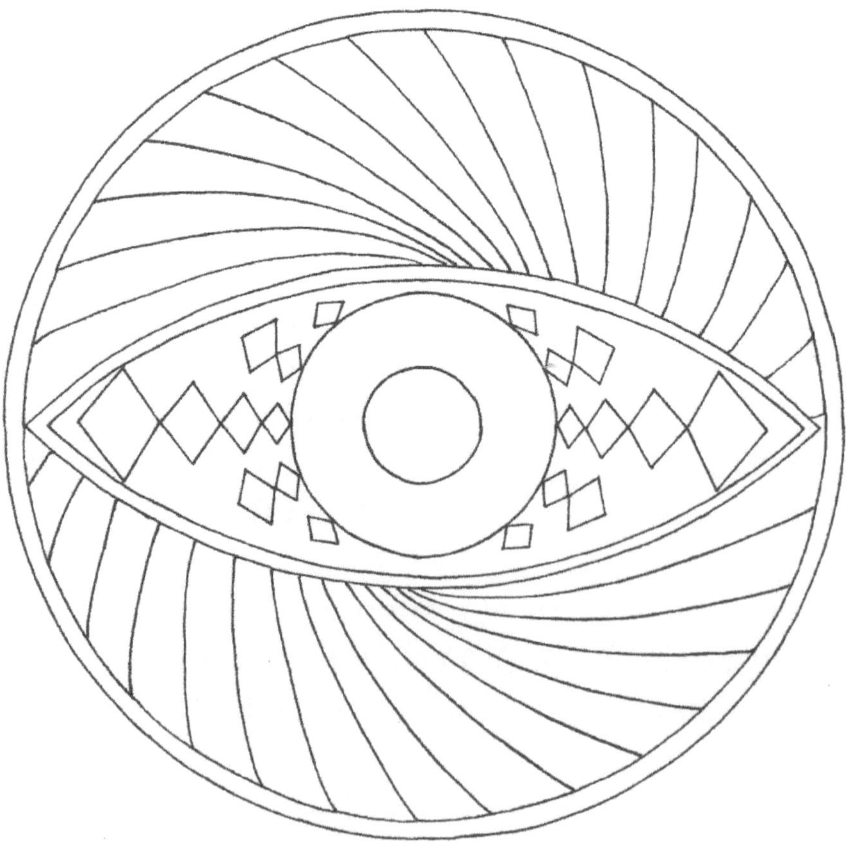

9
FIRE TRUCK

Ray was driving her fire truck today. It made her so happy that she called Baba: "Baba, look I am driving a truck!" she told Him proudly.

"Yes, Ray, I see. You are a big girl! When you grow older it is important to know how to (for your spiritual progress)

Start early
Drive slowly
Reach safely.

The same applies to driving a car. Leave early enough and then drive slowly, not too fast and you will reach your destination safely!"

10
SEE GOOD

Each week Ray and her family visit Grandma. This time Ray is putting grandma's glasses on, and she thinks it is very funny! She wants Baba to see her wearing the glasses.

Baba speaks: "Yes, Ray, you look very grown up wearing these glasses!" He then goes on: "Glasses are needed if your sight is not optimal. It is important to have perfect vision.

But it is more important to **see good, do good and be good**. Only look at good things, do good actions and be a good girl and listen to your parents!"

BABA'S TEACHINGS

All things are beautiful when seen through the eyes of love.

Samastha Loka Sukhino Bhavanthu
Let all the worlds be happy
(and thereby all the beings in the worlds)

It is the inner purity that matters, not the outer movement of lips.

God is inside you.
God is in every word, in every deed, and in every thought of yours.
Speak, do, and think as it befits Him.

Do not use poisonous words against anyone, for words wound more fatally than even arrows.

Give all your burdens to God. Be light and free. Have sacred faith. Without faith, there is no success in life.

Yes, Ray, I am very happy that you love animals, because they are all God's creatures! That is why it is important not to kill animals and eat them. It is cruel.

WATCH	WATCH YOUR WORDS
ACTIONS	WATCH YOUR ACTIONS
THOUGHTS	WATCH YOUR THOUGHTS
CHARACTER	WATCH YOUR CHARACTER
HEART	WATCH YOUR HEART

Start early
Drive slowly
Reach safely.

See good, do good, and be good.

ABOUT THE AUTHOR

Dorothea was born and raised in Switzerland to two nature-loving souls. Therefore, she believes the love for nature is in her genes.

In 1988, she became aware of Sri Sathya Sai Baba and went to India in 1990 for the first time. She took a Mandala Drawing Course in approximately 1990.

After meeting her husband in London, England, they moved to the USA and after that, to Switzerland. They stayed there for twenty years, where all their children were born. She has been residing in Canada since 1997.

9 789367 074978

Printed at Repro India Ltd.